Bear E. Bear

Susan Straight • Illustrated by Marisabina Russo

HYPERION BOOKS FOR CHILDREN
NEW YORK

For Gaila
—S.S.

For Donna
—M.R.

For information address Hyperion Books for Children,
114 Fifth Avenue, New York, New York 10011.

FIRST EDITION
1 3 5 7 9 10 8 6 4 2

Library of Congress Cataloging-in-Publication Data

Straight, Susan
Bear E. Bear/Susan Straight; illustrated by Marisabina Russo — 1st ed.
p.   cm.
Summary: When Gaila's baby sister Delphine drops Bear E. Bear into the
mud, Mama makes sure he gets nice and clean in the washing machine.
ISBN 1-56282-526-7 (trade) — ISBN 1-56282-527-5 (lib. bdg.)
[1. Teddy bears — Fiction.   2. Laundry — Fiction.
3. Family life — Fiction.]   I. Russo, Marisabina, ill.   II. Title.
PZ7.S8955Be   1995
[E] — dc20   94 – 19306   CIP   AC

The artwork for each picture is prepared using gouache.
This book is set in 14.5-point Korinna.

Bear E. Bear

My baby sister dropped Bear E. Bear in the gutter today! Mama picked us up from Grandma's house, where we stay while Mama's at work, and I was getting into my car seat. Delphine tried to grab Bear E. Bear, and he fell out of my arms. He was upside down in the muddy water by the sidewalk.

Mama looked right in my face, and she saw how my eyes felt real hot. She dried off Bear E. Bear's head with a towel and said, "When we get home, we can put him in the washer. He'll like that."

He rode in my lap like always. His fur was spiky on top of his head, like my uncle John's hair. I kept Bear E. Bear away from Delphine, and she chewed on her toes. Mama sang with the radio. I could smell her work perfume.

At home, I sit on the dryer while Mama turns on the washing machine. The waterfall comes down into the big circle of the washer, and Mama lets me pour in the soap from the scooper. She says the water is warm, like my bath. Bear E. Bear doesn't like cold water, and hot water might burn him. I hold him tight, and I can smell the mud, from the gutter, on his head. Mama holds Delphine and lets her drop the clothes in the machine. Then I put Bear E. Bear on top, and the circle starts to squish around.

"Don't you want to get down now?" Mama asks. I tell her I like to sit here on the dryer and watch, with the washer lid up.

Bear E. Bear gets pulled down by the turning of the washer. I can see him go under the soapsuds, but Mama says he'll come right back up. The socks and T-shirts all jump around in the water, and then I see Bear E. Bear's arm. He waves at me, and then I see his nose. Bear E. Bear has a nose that is lighter than the rest of his face. Grandma saw that the strings across his nose were almost gone, and she sewed a thread back and forth across it. His new nose got dirty when Leisha threw him on the ground outside. I picked him up and took him away. She always grabs him, and I get mad.

Leisha comes to Grandma's house when her mama goes to work. She makes fun of Bear E. Bear. She says I'm a baby. But my friend Blaise has NyeNye. NyeNye used to be a blanket, and now it's a corner with fuzzy edges. And his sister Taylor has Fluffy. Her Fluffy used to be a rabbit, and now it's a big piece of fluff.

Bear E. Bear comes back up, and I say hi to him before the water comes over him again. Then the water runs out of the circle and into the big sink in the washroom. Mama's doing the dishes and Daddy comes home. He sees me on the dryer and says, "Bear E. Bear bit the dust again, huh?"

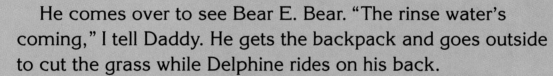

He comes over to see Bear E. Bear. "The rinse water's coming," I tell Daddy. He gets the backpack and goes outside to cut the grass while Delphine rides on his back.

When I was little, I used to ride in the backpack while Daddy cut the grass. Now I'm too big. But I can jump in the trash can to mash down the grass. Today I have to stay here so Bear E. Bear won't be scared.

Mama comes in to close the washer lid so the rinse cycle can work. She shows me the washer cycles at night when we do the laundry. She shows me how bleach goes in with the white clothes and extra detergent goes on the knees of all Delphine's pants.

After a long time, Mama comes to ask, "How's Bear E. Bear?" and we lift up the lid to see. He's done now, smiling up at me from the bottom of the washer. But he's cold.

"Put him in the dryer, okay?" I ask her. When Mama lifts him out of the washer, I take him for a minute. I hold him close while she puts the clothes in the dryer. His wet fur leaves a dark spot on my T-shirt.

"Come on, Gaila," Mama says. "Lay him in there to dry while we eat dinner." I put Bear E. Bear in the big dryer cave and close the door real soft so he won't be scared of the dark.

After dinner Delphine eats some soap in the bathtub. She eats everything. I get out of the bathtub fast tonight so I can check on Bear E. Bear. Mama opens the dryer door, and he is holding a long sock. "He's still damp," Mama says.

"Can't I wait here?" I ask. She smiles and says I can.

I sit on the floor, wrapped in my towel, and I can feel the dryer rumbling by my arm. My cousin Holla said I have lots of bears, so how come I can only sleep with Bear E. Bear? Holla sleeps by herself. I told her I don't know.

But I can't sleep without Bear E. Bear.

One night I left him at Grandpa John's, all the way across town. I cried, and Daddy said, "I'll get him tomorrow after work." But I cried some more, and Mama said, "Come on, Gailagirl." We drove back to Grandpa's. The night was dark, but the streetlights were on. Mama let me sit in the front seat with her, in my seat belt, and she played the radio loud so we could sing. I love being alone with Mama in the car at night. Bear E. Bear sat in the seat belt with me on the way home.

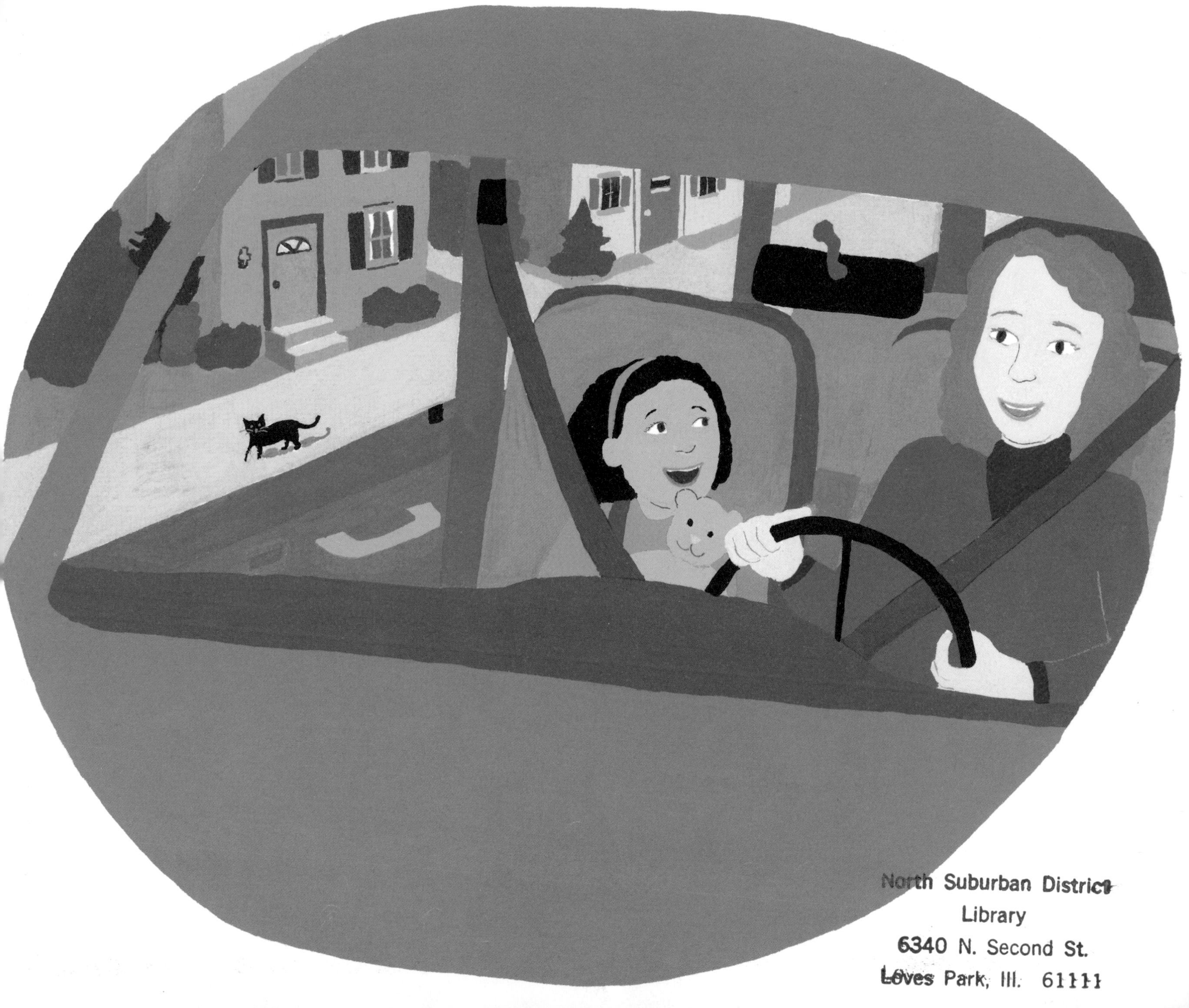

The dryer stops now, and I pull open the door. Bear E. Bear is warm, and his fur is soft again. When he has dried juice on him, his fur gets little dreadlocks, like my cousin Sensei.

But when Bear E. Bear is clean, he's the same color as me. Light brown. Like my mama's tea, for when she's tired. I go to see her in the kitchen, and I show her Bear E. Bear. When she kisses him good-night, I touch her teacup with the flowers on it. Bear E. Bear's eyes are warm, like the cup.

Mama puts us to bed. My daddy's fixing the radio in the car.
My baby sister Delphine is already sleeping in her crib. I hold
Bear E. Bear close under my covers so he won't get cold again.

He stays warm with me. Now I can close my eyes, because
I can still feel his nose on my neck, even in the dark.